BELOW

NINA CREWS

Henry Holt and Company

New York

Henry Holt and Company, LLC
Publishers since 1866
175 Fifth Avenue
New York, New York 10010
www.henryholtchildrensbooks.com

Henry Holt® is a registered trademark of Henry Holt and Company, LLC.
Copyright © 2006 by Nina Crews
All rights reserved.
Distributed in Canada by H. B. Fenn and Company Ltd.

Library of Congress Cataloging-in-Publication Data
Crews, Nina.
Below / Nina Crews.—1st ed.
p.   cm.
Summary: Jack has adventures and rescues with his action figure Guy.
ISBN-13: 978-0-8050-7728-5
ISBN-10: 0-8050-7728-6
[1. Action figures (Toys)—Fiction. 2. Toys—Fiction.] I. Title.
PZ7.C8693Bel 2005   [E]—dc22   2005012128

First Edition—2006
The artist used digitally color-corrected and manipulated 35mm color photographs,
line drawings, and black-and-white photographs to create the illustrations for this book.
Printed in China on acid-free paper. ∞

10 9 8 7 6 5 4 3

To the Raders
— N.C.

Many thanks to Jack Rader, Gus Rader, Amy Crews,
and Todd Rader for participating in this book.
Also thanks to Sam Henriques and Becky Lax
for the use of their stairs.

Jack lived in a tall, narrow house.
A tall, narrow house with many stairs.
Jack climbed up and Jack climbed down.
He always brought Guy with him.
They had many adventures.

Jack and Guy climbed huge mountains.

**Jack and Guy visited vast cities.**

Jack and Guy explored a forest.
They found a hole.
What was in there? they wondered.
Jack was too big to look inside.
Guy was willing to go alone.
So, Jack held Guy over that hole
                              and
                          let
                          go!

Guy tumbled and rattled down, down, down.

"Oh, no!" cried Jack.

Jack looked hard, but he couldn't see Guy.
Would Guy be okay down there?

There might be dragons!

There might be wild horses!

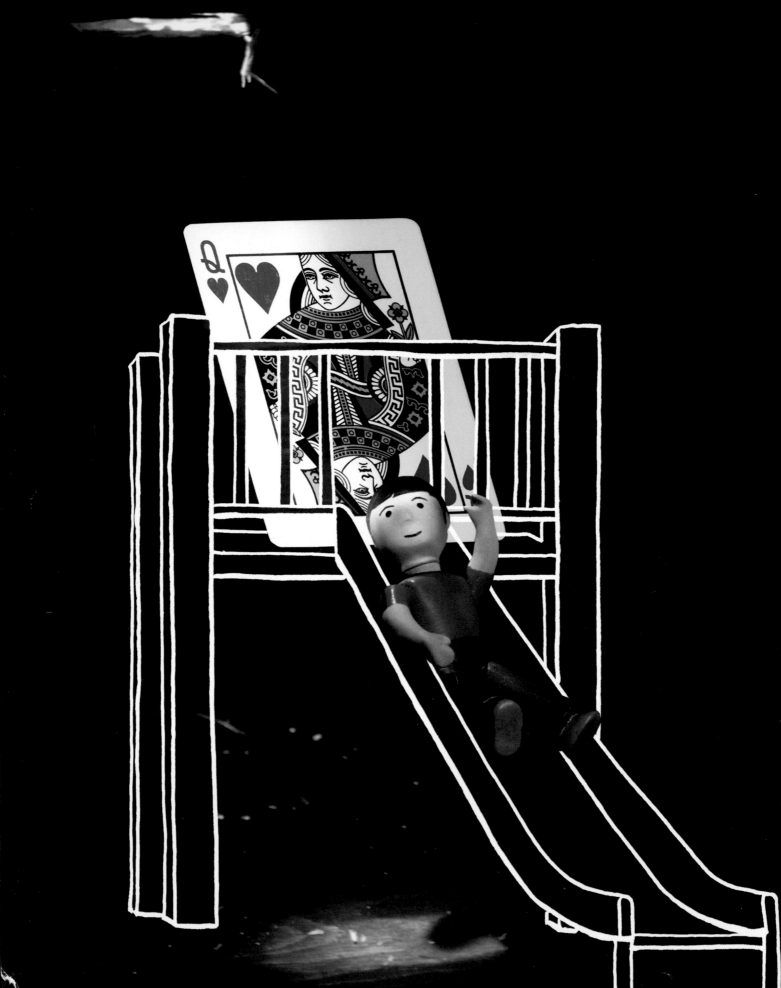

There might be other toys in the hole!

Or Guy might be all alone.

Jack asked his mother
to help him rescue Guy,
but she was busy with Gus.

And Jack's father said,
"I'm fixing this door right now.
I'll help you later."

Jack decided to get Guy himself.
He got his fire truck.
He got his crane and his workmen.
Soon his rescue party was ready to begin.

He took his big crane and lowered
the line down, down, down.

Up came a toy soldier.
Up came a brass button
and a ball of foil lost by the cat.
Up came two pennies and a dime.
Up came Guy!

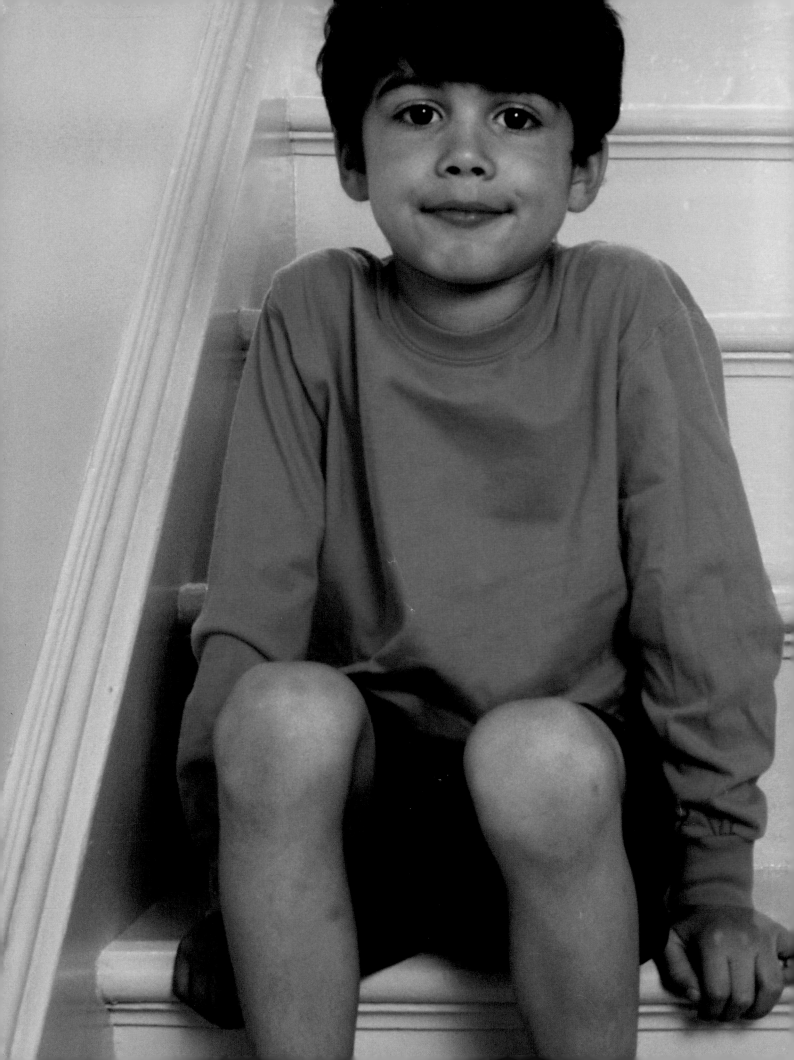

From that day on, whenever
Jack and Guy went exploring,
they stayed together.

But sometimes they wondered
what might be happening below.